UBU ROI

Alfred Jarry

Translated by

Beverly Keith and G. Legman

DOVER PUBLICATIONS, INC.
MINEOLA, NEW YORK

DOVER THRIFT EDITIONS

GENERAL EDITOR: PAUL NEGRI
EDITOR OF THIS VOLUME: DREW SILVER

Copyright

Bibliographical Note

Variations of the text of *Ubu Roi* were published in 1893 and 1894. The text performed at the premiere was first published in 1896. The play was first performed—with scenery painted by Vuillard, Bonnard, Serusier, and Toulouse-Lautrec—in December 1896.

This Dover edition, first published in 2003, is an unabridged republication of the "King Turd" section of *King Turd*, published by Boar's Head Books, New York, in 1953. Translation is by Beverly Keith and G. (Gershon) Legman. The Note was prepared especially for this edition.

Theatrical Rights

This Dover Thrift Edition may be used in its entirety, in adaptation, or in any other way for theatrical productions, professional and amateur, in the United States, without permission, fee, or acknowledgment. (This may not apply outside of the United States, as copyright conditions may vary.)

Library of Congress Cataloging-in-Publication Data

Jarry, Alfred, 1873–1907.
    [Ubu roi. English]
    Ubu Roi / Alfred Jarry ; translated by Beverly Keith and G. Legman.
       p. cm. — (Dover thrift editions)
    ISBN-13: 978-0-486-42687-7 (pbk.)
    ISBN-10: 0-486-42687-4 (pbk.)
      1. Keith, Beverly. II. Legman, G. (Gershon), 1917– III. Title.

PQ2619.A65 U313 2003
842'.8—dc21

                                      2002034821

Manufactured in the United States by Courier Corporation
42687406   2014
www.doverpublications.com

NOTE

The original production of *Ubu roi ou les polonais* (*King Ubu or the Poles*) was staged December 9, 1896 (a dress rehearsal before an invited audience), and December 10 (the premiere and, as it turned out, last performance). Commotion, though not quite the "riots" of legend—arguments, shouted insults, puzzled or annoyed departures—broke out at both performances. Accounts of the production sometimes confuse or conflate the events of the two nights, but all agree that they were memorable evenings in the theater.

Ubu Roi derived from a precocious satire by the teenaged Jarry and some school friends. Its various sources may also include *Macbeth*, the character of the politician Thiers, Shakespeare's *Titus Andronicus*, Chabrier's *Le roi malgré lui*, Brillat-Savarin's *Physiologie du goût*, and undoubtedly others. It is a preposterous farce, an anarchic parody, an energetically violent and scatological gesture against propriety, smugness, and stupidity in general, as well as against the tame theatrical conventions of the time. The character Ubu originated as a burlesque of a much unloved teacher, the unfortunate M. Hébert, a fat, ineffectual professor at the lycée at Rennes, who later became a reactionary local politician. Over the years Jarry worked on the play, Ubu came to embody every despicable quality: he is pompous, vain, cruel, stupid, murderous, cowardly, greedy, and authoritarian—altogether an exemplary authority figure.

Ubu Roi's literary significance lies in its poetic quality. Its uninhibited tastelessness is practically sublime, and it is a lot funnier than *Hamlet* (another possible source), in which corpses also pile up. For the Théâtre de l'Oeuvre, which mounted the 1896 production, *Ubu Roi* was, in Steegmuller's words, "the catastrophe that made it famous." The occasion became legendary, a high point of the pre-1914 avant-garde.

vi

Alfred Jarry (1873–1907), writer, philosopher, pistol-packing midget bicyclist, was a prominent, strangely beloved figure in the advanced artistic and literary circles of Paris from the mid-1890s until his death. Only twenty three when *Ubu* was staged, Jarry went on to create a corpus of straight-faced comic essays, plays, poems, novels, and speculative philosophical prose. Among his better known works today are the second and third plays of the Ubu cycle, *Ubu Enchaîné* (*Ubu Bound*, 1900) and *Ubu Cocu* (*Ubu Cuckolded*, 1901); the collection *Minutes de sable mémorial* (1894); the novels *Les jours et les nuits* (1897) and *Le surmâle*, 1902; *Gestes et opinions du docteur Faustroll, pataphysicien* (1898, published 1911); and the famous essay "How to Construct a Time Machine" (1900). He has been seen as an ancestor of Dada, Futurism, Surrealism, Artaud's Theater of Cruelty, the Theater of the Absurd, even of Brecht, and continues to influence artists, writers, and thinkers today.

*   *   *

The present translators have chosen to render the title character's name as "King Turd," which is certainly in keeping with the grossness of his character and the language of the play, but the reader should know that "Ubu" is in origin a nonsense word, not specifically scatological. (The derivative "Ubuesque," has come to mean, in French and English, "ludicrous" or "absurd.")

As Jarry explains in his curtain speech, the action of *Ubu Roi* "takes place in Poland—that is to say, nowhere." This is not a Polish joke but a reference, in 1896, to the Polish state's nonexistence, having been wiped off the map a hundred years before after a series of partitions by its more powerful neighbors.

The illustrations that accompany the text, including the frontispiece, are by Jarry himself.

PREFACE

[*Spoken by Jarry before the curtain at the first performance of* UBU ROI *at the Théâtre de l'Oeuvre, Paris,* 10 *December* 1896.]

Ladies and Gentlemen : It would be superfluous – aside from a certain absurdity in an author's speaking of his own play – for me to come here and preface with a few words this presentation of UBU ROI, after such famous critics have cared to discuss it : among whom I must thank – and with these few all the others – MM. Silvestre, Mendès, Scholl, Lorrain and Bauer ; if I did not feel that their benevolence had found Ubu's belly big with more satirical symbols than we can possibly pump up tonight.

The Swedenborgian philosopher, Mésès, has excellently compared rudimentary creations with the most perfect, and embryonic beings with the most complete, in that the former lack all irregularities, protuberances and qualities, which leaves them in more or less spherical form, like the ovum and M. Ubu, while the latter have added so many personal details that they remain equally spherical, following the axiom that the most polished object is that which presents the greatest number of sharp corners. That is why you are free to see in M. Ubu however many allusions you care to, or else a simple puppet – a schoolboy's caricature of one of his professors who personified for him all the ugliness in the world. It is this aspect that the Théâtre de l'Oeuvre will present tonight.

Our actors have been willing to depersonalize themselves for two evenings, and to act behind masks, in order to express more perfectly the inner man, the soul of these overgrown

1

puppets you are about to see. The play having been put on
prematurely, and with more enthusiasm than anything else,
Ubu hasn't had time to get his real mask – which is very in-
convenient to wear anyway – and the other characters will
be fitted out, like him, somewhat approximately.

It seemed very important, if we were to be quite like puppets (Ubu Roi is a play that was never written for puppets,
but for actors pretending to be puppets, which is not the
same thing), for us to have carnival music, and the orchestral
parts have been allotted to various brasses, gongs and speak-
ing-trumpet horns that we haven't had time to collect. We
don't hold it too much against the Théâtre de l'Oeuvre.
Mainly we wanted to see Ubu incarnate in the versatile talent
of M. Gémier, and tonight and tomorrow night are the only
two performances that M. Ginisty and his production of Vil-
liers de l'Isle-Adam have been free to relinquish to us.

We will proceed with the three acts that have been rehearsed, and two that have been rehearsed with certain cuts.
I have made all the cuts the actors wanted, even cutting several passages indispensable to the meaning and equilibrium
of the play, while leaving in at their request certain scenes
I would have been glad to cut. For however much we'd like
to be marionnettes, we haven't hung all our actors on strings,
which, even if it weren't absurd, would have complicated
things badly. In the same way, we haven't been too literal
about our crowd scenes, whereas in a puppet-show a handful
of strings and pulleys will serve to command a whole army.
You must expect to see important personages like M. Ubu
and the Czar forced to gallop neck-and-neck on cardboard
horses that we've spent the night painting in order to supply
the action. The first three acts, at least, and the final scenes,
will be played complete, as they were written.

Our stage setting is very appropriate, because even though
it's an easy trick to lay your scene in eternity, and, for in-
stance, to have someone shoot off a revolver in the year one-
thousand-and-such, here you must accept doors that open

out on plains covered with snow falling from a clear sky, chimneys adorned with clocks splitting open to serve as doors, and palm-trees growing at the foot of bedsteads for little elephants sitting on shelves to munch on. As to our orchestra that isn't here, we'll miss only its brilliance and tone. The themes for UBU will be performed offstage by various pianos and drums. As to the action which is about to begin, it takes place in Poland – that is to say, nowhere.

COMPOSITION

OF

THE ORCHESTRA

Oboes

Pipes

Sausages

Big Bass

Flageolets

Transverse Flutes

Grand Flute

Little Bassoon

Big Bassoon

Shrill white Trumpets

Triple Bassoon

Little black Trumpets

Horns

Sackbutts

Trombones

Green Oliphants

Fipple-flutes

Bagpipes

Tubas

Kettledrums

Drum

Bass Drum

Grand Organ

CHARACTERS

PAPA TURD
MAMA TURD
CAPTAIN BORDURE
KING WENCESLAUS
QUEEN ROSAMUNDE
BOLESLAUS
LADISLAUS } *their sons*
BUGGERLAUS
THE GHOSTS OF THEIR ANCESTORS
GENERAL LASKY
STANISLAS LECZINSKI
JAN SOBIESKI

NICHOLAS RENSKY

THE EMPEROR ALEXIS

GYRON

PILE   } *Champions*

COCCYX

CONSPIRATORS AND SOLDIERS

PEOPLE

MICHAEL FEODOROVITCH

NOBLES

MAGISTRATES

COUNCILLORS

FINANCIERS

LACKEYS OF PHYNANCE

PEASANTS

THE WHOLE RUSSIAN ARMY

THE WHOLE POLISH ARMY

THE GUARDS OF MAMA TURD

A CAPTAIN

THE BEAR

THE MONEY-GO-MARE

THE DEBRAINING MACHINE

THE CREW

THE SEA-CAPTAIN

THIS BOOK
IS DEDICATED
TO
MARCEL SCHWOB

y thenne Papa Turd
shooke the peare-tree
long sithens named
SHAKES-PEARE by yᵉ
Englysshe, and under
thatte name hadd frō
it manie ffine maniu-
script tragædies.

UBU ROI
OR
THE POLES

UBU ROI

ACT I

SCENE I

[Poland – that is to say, nowhere.]

PAPA TURD, MAMA TURD

PAPA TURD. Pshit !

MAMA TURD. Oh ! that's a fine thing. What a pig you are, Papa Turd !

PAPA TURD. Watch out I don't kill you, Mama Turd !

MAMA TURD. It isn't me you ought to kill, Papa Turd, it's someone else.

PAPA TURD. Now by my green candle, I don't understand.

MAMA TURD. What ! Papa Turd, you're content with your lot ?

PAPA TURD. Now by my green candle, pshit, Madam, certainly yes, I'm content. I could be content with less. After all, I'm Captain of Dragoons, Privy Councillor to King Wenceslaus, Knight of the Red Eagle of Poland, and formerly King of Aragon. What more do you want ?

MAMA TURD. What ! After being King of Aragon, you can settle down to reviewing fifty flunkies armed with cabbage-cutters, when you could put the crown of Poland on your head where the crown of Aragon used to be ?

PAPA TURD. Ah, Mama Turd, I don't understand a word you're saying.

11

MAMA TURD. You are so stupid.

PAPA TURD. Now by my green candle, King Wenceslaus is still alive. And suppose he croaks – hasn't he got loads of children ?

MAMA TURD. What prevents you from massacring the whole family and putting yourself in their place ?

PAPA TURD. Ah ! Mama Turd, you do me wrong. Watch out you don't end up in the soup.

MAMA TURD. Poor unfortunate, when I'm in the soup who'll patch the seat of your pants ?

PAPA TURD. Is that so ! And if you don't, then what ? Isn't my ass just like everybody else's ?

MAMA TURD. If I were in your place, that ass – I'd want to plant on a throne. You could make lots of money, and eat all the sausages you want, and roll through the streets in a carriage.

PAPA TURD. If I were King, I'd have a big wide-brimmed hat, the kind I had in Aragon, the one those dirty Spaniards went and stole.

MAMA TURD. You could even get yourself a great big umbrella and a magnificent cape that would hang to your heels.

PAPA TURD. Ah ! I yield to temptation. Buggerly pshit, pshitterly bugger, if I ever run into him in a corner of the woods, I'll give him a bad half hour !

MAMA TURD. Good, Papa Turd ! Now you're talking like a man.

PAPA TURD. No, no ! Me – Captain of Dragoons – massacre the King of Poland ? I'd sooner die !

MAMA TURD (aside). Oh, pshit ! – (Aloud.) So you're going to stay poor as a rat, Papa Turd ?

PAPA TURD. Bluebelly ! by my green candle, I'd rather be poor as a thin honest rat than rich like a wicked fat cat.

MAMA TURD. And the broad-brimmed hat ? And the umbrella ? And the great cape ?

PAPA TURD. And then what, Mama Turd ?

[*He leaves, banging the door.*

MAMA TURD (*alone*). Pfft, pshit ! He isn't very quick on the trigger, but pfft, pshit ! I believe I've got him stirred up just the same. Thanks to God and myself, in a week I may be Queen of Poland.

SCENE II

A room in the house of Papa Turd.
A sumptuous table is set.

PAPA TURD, MAMA TURD

MAMA TURD. Well ! our guests are certainly late.

PAPA TURD. Yes, by my green candle. And I'm dying of hunger. Mama Turd, you're very ugly today. Is that because we're having company ?

MAMA TURD (*shrugging her shoulders*). Pshit !

PAPA TURD (*seizing a roast chicken*). Hey, I'm hungry. I'm going to dig into this bird. Chicken, I suppose. Not bad.

MAMA TURD. What are you doing, you wretch ! What will our guests eat ?

PAPA TURD. They'll still have plenty. I won't take any more . . . Mama Turd, go look out the window and see if our guests are coming.

MAMA TURD (*going to the window*). I don't see anyone. (*Meanwhile* PAPA TURD *snitches a roast of veal.*) Ah ! there's Captain Bordure arriving with his men. What are you eating now, Papa Turd ?

PAPA TURD. Nothing, a bit of veal.

MAMA TURD. Oh ! the veal ! the veal ! Veal ! He's eaten the veal ! Help !

PAPA TURD. Now by my green candle, I'm going to scratch your eyes out.

(*The door opens.*)

SCENE III

PAPA TURD, MAMA TURD, CAPTAIN BORDURE *and his* MEN

MAMA TURD. Good day, gentlemen, we've been waiting for you impatiently. Pray be seated.

CAPTAIN BORDURE. Good day, Madam. But where is Papa Turd?

PAPA TURD. Where am I? Here I am, dammit! By my green candle, I'm certainly fat enough.

BORDURE. Hello, Papa Turd. Sit down, men.

[*They all sit.*

PAPA TURD. Oof! any more and I'd go through the chair.

BORDURE. Well, Mama Turd, what have you got that's good today?

MAMA TURD. Here's the menu.

PAPA TURD. Oh, this interests me.

MAMA TURD. Potato soup, drat chops, veal, chicken, dog-paste, turkey rumps, charlotte russe . . .

PAPA TURD. All right, that's enough. – You mean to say there's more?

MAMA TURD (*continuing*). Sherbet, salad, fruit, dessert, boiled beef, Jerusalem artichokes, cauliflower à la pshit.

PAPA TURD. Hey! you think I'm an Oriental potentate, spending all that money?

MAMA TURD. Don't listen to him, he's an imbecile.

PAPA TURD. I'm going to sharpen my teeth on your calves.

MAMA TURD. Eat your dinner instead, Papa Turd. Here's some potato soup.

PAPA TURD. Buggery, but it's bad!

BORDURE. It isn't terribly good, as a matter of fact.

MAMA TURD. You bunch of savages, what do you want?

PAPA TURD (*hitting himself on the forehead*). Wait! I have an idea. I'll be right back.   [*He goes out.*

MAMA TURD. Gentlemen, will you try some veal?

BORDURE. It's very good. I'm through.

MAMA TURD. And now the rumps.

BORDURE. Delicious! delicious! Hurray for Mama Turd!

ALL. Hurray for Mama Turd!

PAPA TURD (*returning*). And soon you'll be shouting "Hurray for Papa Turd!" (*In his hand he holds an unmentionable mop. He dashes it on the banqueting table.*)

MAMA TURD. Wretch! what are you doing?

PAPA TURD. Try a little of that. (*Several taste it and fall down poisoned.*) – Mama Turd, pass me the drat chops. I'll serve.

MAMA TURD. Here they are.

PAPA TURD. All right, everybody outside! Out! Captain Bordure, I want to talk to you.

THE OTHERS. Hey! we haven't eaten.

PAPA TURD. Whaddya mean, you haven't eaten? Everybody outside! You stay, Bordure. (*No one budges.*) – Not gone yet? Now by my green candle, I'm going to murder you with these drat chops. (*He begins throwing them.*)

ALL. Ooh! Ouch! Help! Defend yourselves! Curses! I'm dead!

PAPA TURD. Pshit, pshit, pshit! Outside! You hear me?

ALL. Save yourselves! Miserable Papa Turd! Cheap double-crossing skunk!

PAPA TURD. There! they're gone. I can relax now, but I didn't get much to eat. Come, Bordure.

[*They leave with* MAMA TURD.

SCENE IV

PAPA TURD, MAMA TURD, CAPTAIN BORDURE

PAPA TURD. Well then, Captain, did you dine well?

CAPTAIN BORDURE. Pretty well, sir, except for the pshit.

PAPA TURD. Eh! the pshit wasn't bad.

MAMA TURD. Tastes differ.

PAPA TURD. Captain Bordure, I've decided to make you Duke of Lithuania.

BORDURE. But how ? I thought you were terribly poor, Papa Turd.

PAPA TURD. In a few days, if you please, I shall reign over Poland.

BORDURE. You're going to kill Wenceslaus ?

PAPA TURD. He's not so dumb, the bugger. He guessed it.

BORDURE. If it's a question of killing Wenceslaus, I'm in. I'm his mortal enemy and I'll answer for my men.

PAPA TURD (*throwing himself on* BORDURE *to kiss him*). Oh ! oh ! I love you, Bordure.

BORDURE. Ugh ! you stink, Papa Turd. Don't you ever wash ?

PAPA TURD. Rarely.

MAMA TURD. Never !

PAPA TURD. I'm going to stamp on your feet !

MAMA TURD. Big pshit !

PAPA TURD. Go, Bordure, I've finished with you. But by my green candle, I swear by Mama Turd to make you Duke of Lithuania.

MAMA TURD. But . . .

PAPA TURD. Shut up, my sweet child . . .

[*They go out.*

SCENE V

PAPA TURD, MAMA TURD, A MESSENGER

PAPA TURD. What do you want, mister ? Shag off, you annoy me.

THE MESSENGER. You are summoned, Sir, by the King.

[*He goes out.*

PAPA TURD. Oh ! pshit, bloodyblueblazes, by my green candle, he's found out ! I'm going to have my head cut off ! Oh ! Oh !!

MAMA TURD. What a weakling ! And time is short.

PAPA TURD. Oh ! I have an idea : I'll say it was Mama Turd and Bordure.

MAMA TURD. You big P.U. . . . you do that, and . . .

PAPA TURD. Ha ! That's just what I'll do.   [*He goes out.*

MAMA TURD (*running after him*). Oh, Papa Turd, Papa Turd ! I'll give you sausages !

PAPA TURD (*offstage*). Pshit ! You know what you can do with your sausages !

SCENE VI

A hall in the palace at Warsaw.

KING WENCESLAUS, *surrounded by his* OFFICERS, BORDURE, *the king's sons*, BOLESLAUS, LADISLAUS, *and* BUGGERLAUS. *Then* TURD.

PAPA TURD (*entering*). It wasn't me, you know ! It was Mama Turd and Bordure.

THE KING. What is the matter, Papa Turd ?

BORDURE. He's been drinking.

THE KING. Ah yes, like me, this morning.

PAPA TURD. That's it, I'm drunk. I've been drinking too much adequate little French wine.

THE KING. Papa Turd, I must reward you for your numerous services as Captain of Dragoons, and so today I dub you Count of Sandomir.

PAPA TURD. O Sire Wenceslaus, I don't know how to thank you.

THE KING. Don't thank me, Papa Turd. Be on hand tomorrow at the full-dress parade.

PAPA TURD. I'll be there, but – as a favor to me – accept this little reed flute. (*He gives the king a flute.*)

THE KING. What would a man my age do with a flute ? I'll give it to young Buggerlaus.

YOUNG BUGGERLAUS. Oh, is Papa Turd stupid !

PAPA TURD. Well, I guess I'll bugger off. (*He falls down turning away.*) Oh ! Ow ! Help ! By my green candle, I've busted a gut and cracked my bumbazine !

THE KING (*picking him up*). Did you hurt yourself, Papa Turd ?

PAPA TURD. Of course, and I'm sure to croak. What will become of Mama Turd ?

THE KING. We shall see to her maintenance.

PAPA TURD. You're very kind. (*He goes out.*) – Yes, but King Wenceslaus, all the same you're going to be massacred.

SCENE VII

Turd's house.

GYRON, PILE, *and* COCCYX ; PAPA TURD, MAMA TURD,
CONSPIRATORS *and* SOLDIERS, CAPTAIN BORDURE

PAPA TURD. Well, my dear friends, it's high time we decided on a plan of action. Everybody'll give their opinion, I'll give mine first, if you don't mind.

BORDURE. Speak, Papa Turd.

PAPA TURD. Well then, my friends, my idea is simply to poison the king by sticking arsenic in his breakfast. Then when he goes to chomp on it, he'll drop dead, and so I'll be king.

ALL. Pfui ! What a swine !

PAPA TURD. What ? You don't like it ? All right, let's hear Bordure's idea.

BORDURE. I think we should strike him a terrible blow of the sword, and split him open from head to tail.

ALL. Fine ! That's noble ! That's the manly thing.

PAPA TURD. And what if he starts kicking you ? I just remembered – on parade he wears iron boots, and they really hurt. If I had thought of that before, I'd've gone and denounced the bunch of you for dragging me into this mess. I'll bet I'd get a reward too.

MAMA TURD. Oh ! the traitor, the coward, the scaly, scurvy son of a bitch !

ALL. Vomit on Papa Turd !

PAPA TURD. Listen, you fellows, just keep calm if you don't want a couple of black eyes. I'll tell you what – I'm willing to take the risk for you. Let's see now. Bordure, it'll be your job to split the king down the middle.

BORDURE. Wouldn't it be better for us all to jump on him at once, yelling and screaming ? That way we'd have a better chance of winning over the troops.

PAPA TURD. Now look, I'll go to step on his feet. He'll jump back, and I'll say to him : PSHIT, and that's the signal for the bunch of you to jump on him.

MAMA TURD. Yes, and as soon as he's dead, you grab his sceptre and crown.

BORDURE. And I'll go after the royal family with my men.

PAPA TURD. Yes. And be sure to get that little Buggerlaus.

[*They troop out.*

PAPA TURD (*running after them, and bringing them back*). Gentlemen, we forgot an indispensable part of the ceremony. We have to swear to fight valiantly.

BORDURE. But what can we swear on? We haven't any priest.

PAPA TURD. Mama Turd will do instead.

ALL. All right. Let's go.

PAPA TURD. So do you swear to kill the king good?

ALL. Yes! We swear. Up with Papa Turd!

ACT II

SCENE I

The King's palace.

KING WENCESLAUS, QUEEN ROSAMUNDE, BOLESLAUS, LADISLAUS *and* BUGGERLAUS, *Princes*

THE KING. Prince Buggerlaus, you were very impertinent this morning to Master Turd, chevalier of my orders and Count of Sandomir. Therefore I forbid you to appear at our parade.

THE QUEEN. But Wenceslaus, it wouldn't be a bit too much for you to have your whole family protecting you.

THE KING. Madam, I never change my mind. You tire me with these trifles.

BUGGERLAUS. My father, I submit.

THE QUEEN. Really, Sire, do you still insist on going to that parade?

THE KING. And why not, Madam?

THE QUEEN. Why not!? Haven't I dreamed again of him smiting you with his horde of troops and throwing you into the Vistula, while an eagle like that on the arms of Poland sets the crown upon his head?

THE KING. Whose head?

THE QUEEN. Papa Turd's!

THE KING. What nonsense! Master van Turd is a very fine gentleman. He would let himself be torn apart by wild horses to serve me.

THE QUEEN *and* BUGGERLAUS. What folly!

THE KING. Be still, you young swine. And as for you, Madam, to show how little fear I have of Master Turd, I will go on review as I am, with neither sword nor buckler.

21

THE QUEEN. Fatal daring! I shall never see you more.

THE KING. Come, Ladislaus. Come, Boleslaus. [*They leave.*

(THE QUEEN *and* BUGGERLAUS *go to the window.*)

THE QUEEN *and* BUGGERLAUS. May God and great Saint Nicholas protect you!

THE QUEEN. Buggerlaus, come with me to the chapel to pray for your father and your brothers.

SCENE II

The parade-ground.

THE POLISH ARMY, THE KING, BOLESLAUS, LADISLAUS, PAPA TURD, CAPTAIN BORDURE *and his men*; GYRON, PILE, *and* COCCYX.

THE KING. Noble Papa Turd, come closer with your suite, and we will inspect the troops.

PAPA TURD (*to his men*). Look sharp, you fellows. – (*To* THE KING). Coming, Sir, coming. (TURD'S *men surround* THE KING.)

THE KING. Ah! there is my regiment of Dantziger horse-guards. My word, aren't they fine!

PAPA TURD. You think so? They look awful to me. Look at that guy. – (*To* THE SOLDIER). How long since you took a shave, you dirty bum?

THE KING. But this soldier is quite proper, Papa Turd. What is the matter with you?

PAPA TURD. That! (*He stamps on* THE KING's *foot.*)

THE KING. Wretch!

PAPA TURD. PSHIT! Come on, men!

BORDURE. Hurrah! Forward! (*All strike* THE KING. A CLOWN *explodes.*)

THE KING. Ah! Help! Holy Virgin, I'm dead!

BOLESLAUS (*to* LADISLAUS). What's up? Draw your sword.

PAPA TURD [*rolling* THE KING *to the front of the stage with a stick.* – Is he dead yet ? No ? So much the worse ! (*Gives him the finishing stroke.*) – Now I'm king !] Ha ! I have the crown ! Now for the others.

BORDURE. Death to the traitors !!

[*The king's sons flee. All pursue them.*

SCENE III

THE QUEEN, BUGGERLAUS

THE QUEEN. At last I begin to feel reassured.

BUGGERLAUS. You have absolutely nothing to fear.

(*A horrible clamor is heard outside.*)

THE QUEEN. What is that dreadful noise ?

BUGGERLAUS. Oh ! What do I see ? My two brothers, with Papa Turd and his men chasing them.

THE QUEEN. Oh my God ! Holy Virgin, they're losing – they're losing ground.

BUGGERLAUS. The whole army is following Papa Turd. Where's the king ? Horrors ! Help !

THE QUEEN. Oh dear, Boleslaus is dead ! He's been hit by a bullet.

BUGGERLAUS. Hey ! (LADISLAUS *turns.*) Defend yourself ! Hurray for Ladislaus !

THE QUEEN. Oh ! he's surrounded.

BUGGERLAUS. He's done for. Bordure just cut him in half like a sausage.

THE QUEEN. Alas ! These madmen are breaking into the palace. They're coming up the stairs.

(*The clamor increases.*)

THE QUEEN *and* BUGGERLAUS (*on their knees*). *Hospody pomilui* . . .

BUGGERLAUS. Oh, that Papa Turd ! That miserable louse ! If I had him here —

SCENE IV

THE SAME. *The door is broken down.* PAPA TURD
and his partisans burst in.

PAPA TURD. Go on, Buggerlaus, what would you do?

BUGGERLAUS. God almighty! I will defend my mama to the death! The first one that takes a step forward dies like a dog!

PAPA TURD. Oh, Bordure, I'm scared! Let me out of here.

A SOLDIER (*advances*). Buggerlaus, surrender!

BUGGERLAUS. Why, you dog! Here's your come-uppance! (*He bashes in* THE SOLDIER'S *skull.*)

THE QUEEN. That's it, Buggerlaus! Give it to them!

MANY (*advancing*). Buggerlaus, we promise to spare your life.

BUGGERLAUS. Blackguards, rumpots, mercenary swine! (*He makes a windmill with his sword, and massacres them.*)

PAPA TURD. Dammit! I'll finish this thing off just the same.

BUGGERLAUS. Mother, save yourself by the secret staircase.

THE QUEEN. And you, my son, and you?

BUGGERLAUS. I'll follow.

PAPA TURD. Try and catch the queen! Shucks, there she goes! As for you, louse . . . (*He advances toward* BUGGERLAUS.)

BUGGERLAUS. Ah, God almighty! Here is my revenge! (*He rips open* PAPA TURD'S *guts with a terrible blow of his sword.*) Mother, I follow you!

[*He disappears by the secret staircase.*

SCENE V

A cavern in the mountains.

YOUNG BUGGERLAUS *enters,*
followed by QUEEN ROSAMUNDE

BUGGERLAUS. Here we will be safe.

THE QUEEN. Yes, I hope so. Oh, my husband! My darling Wenceslaus! I feel faint. Buggerlaus, support me! (*She falls in the snow.*)

BUGGERLAUS. What ails you, mother dear?

THE QUEEN. I'm very sick, I fear, Buggerlaus. I have only a few hours to live.

BUGGERLAUS. What! have you caught cold?

THE QUEEN. How can I bear up under so many blows? The king massacred, our family destroyed, and you – heir of the noblest race that ever carried dagger – forced to take refuge in the mountains like a common smuggler.

BUGGERLAUS. And by who, great God, by who? A vulgar Papa Turd, an adventurer come from no-one-knows-where, a vile toad, a stinking bum! And when I think that my father decorated him and made him a count, and the very next day that villain had no more shame than to lay violent hands on him.

THE QUEEN. Oh, Buggerlaus, when I remember how happy we were before we ever saw that Papa Turd! But now, alas, everything is changed.

BUGGERLAUS. What's to be done? We can only hope and pray, and never renounce our claim.

THE QUEEN. I hope you get it, my child, but as for me, I shall never see that happy day.

BUGGERLAUS. Eh? what's wrong? She pales, she falls. Help! – But I'm in the wilderness! Oh, my God! Her heart no longer beats. She's dead! Is it possible? Another victim for Papa Turd! (*He buries his face in his hands, and weeps.*)

Oh, my God ! how sad it is to find oneself alone at the age of fourteen, with a terrible vengeance to pursue ! (*He falls prey to the most violent despair. Meanwhile the Souls of* KING WENCESLAUS, BOLESLAUS, LADISLAUS, *and* QUEEN ROSA-MUNDE *enter the grotto, their* ANCESTORS *accompanying them and filling it. The eldest approaches* BUGGERLAUS *and rouses him gently.*) – Eh ! what do I see ? My whole family, my ancestors ! By what miracle . . . ?

THE GHOST. Buggerlaus, I am thy forefather's ghost. In life I was Junkherr Matthias von Koenigsberg, the first king – and founder – of our house. To your hands I entrust our vengeance. (*He gives him a big sword.*) Let this sword that I give you see no rest until it has banged hell out of the usurper. (*The Ghosts disappear, and* BUGGERLAUS *is left, on his knees – brandishing the sword – in an attitude of ecstasy.*)

SCENE VI

The King's palace.

PAPA TURD, MAMA TURD, CAPTAIN BORDURE

PAPA TURD. No ! I won't do it ! You want to ruin me with this nonsense ?

BORDURE. But I say, Papa Turd, don't you know, the people expect gifts, to celebrate your coronation.

MAMA TURD. If you don't distribute food and gold, you'll be overthrown within two hours.

PAPA TURD. Food, yes. Gold, no ! Slaughter up three old nags. That's good enough for such swine.

MAMA TURD. Swine, yourself ! How did I ever get saddled with such a brute ?

PAPA TURD. I'm telling you again : I'm here to get rich. I won't let go of a penny.

MAMA TURD. When he has in his hands all the treasures of Poland.

BORDURE. Wait a minute ! I know where there's an immense treasure hidden in the chapel. We'll distribute that.

PAPA TURD. You bastard ! You do that, and . . .

BORDURE. But Papa Turd, if you don't make any distributions, the people can't pay their taxes.

PAPA TURD. Is that right ?

MAMA TURD. Yes, yes !

PAPA TURD. Oh, well, in that case I consent to everything. Get up three millions, and roast a hundred and fifty cows and sheep, especially seeing that I'm going to have some too.

[*They go out.*

SCENE VII

The palace courtyard, full of people.

PAPA TURD, *wearing the crown,* MAMA TURD, CAPTAIN BORDURE, LACKEYS *loaded with food.*

PEOPLE. There's the king ! Hurray for the king ! Hooray !!

PAPA TURD (*throwing them gold*). Here, catch. This is for you. It don't amuse me much to be throwing away gold, but Mama Turd insisted. At least promise to be sure and pay your taxes.

ALL. Sure, sure !

BORDURE. Look, Mama Turd, see how they fight for the gold. What a battle !

MAMA TURD. It's absolutely horrible. Pfui ! there's one got his head broken.

PAPA TURD. Hey, this is fun. Roll out another barrel of gold.

BORDURE. If we were to have a race . . .

PAPA TURD. Say, that's an idea. (*To the people.*) My friends, you see this barrel ? Inside there's three hundred thousand rose-nobles in gold, coin of the Polish realm, good weight. Everybody that wants to race for it, go stand at that end of the courtyard. You start running when I wave my handkerchief, and the winner gets the barrel. As for those that don't win, they get this other barrel to split up for a booby prize.

ALL. Great! Hurray for Papa Turd! What a good king! Nothing like this ever happened under Wenceslaus.

PAPA TURD (*to* MAMA TURD, *happily*). You hear them? (*All the people line up at the far end of the courtyard.*) One, two, three . . . You ready?

ALL. Yes! Yes!

PAPA TURD. Go!

> (*They start running; tumbling and somer-
> saulting. Cries and tumult.*)

BORDURE. Here they come! Here they come!

PAPA TURD. Oh! the one in front is losing ground.

MAMA TURD. No! now he's ahead.

BORDURE. He's losing, he's losing! All over! It's the other one!

> (*The one that was second finishes first.*)

ALL. Hurray for Michael Feodorovitch! Hurray for Michael Feodorovitch!

MICHAEL FEODOROVITCH. Sire, I honestly don't know how to thank Your Majesty . . .

PAPA TURD. Oh, my dear friend, it's nothing. Take home your barrel of gold, Michael; and as for the rest of you, divide up that other barrel. Everybody take one piece at a time until there aren't any left.

ALL. Hurray for Michael Feodorovitch! Long live Papa Turd!

PAPA TURD. And now, my friends, come and eat. Today I throw open the gates of my palace. Will you do me the honors of my table?

PEOPLE. Let's go! Let's go! Long live Papa Turd! He's the best king of all!

> (*They enter the palace. The noise of their
> orgy continues till morning.
> The curtain falls.*)

ACT III

SCENE I

The palace.

PAPA TURD, MAMA TURD

PAPA TURD. Now, by my green candle, here I am, king in this country. I already have a magnificent indigestion, and pretty soon they're going to bring in my great big cape.

MAMA TURD. What's it made of, Papa Turd? It's all very well to be king, but we have to economize.

PAPA TURD. Madam my female, the cape is made of sheepskin with a clasp and frogs of dog-hide.

MAMA TURD. Why, that's lovely. But it's even lovelier to be king.

PAPA TURD. Yes, you were right all along, Mama Turd.

MAMA TURD. We owe a great deal to the Duke of Lithuania.

PAPA TURD. To who?

MAMA TURD. Why, Captain Bordure.

PAPA TURD. Do me a favor, Mama Turd: don't talk to me about that dummy. Now that I don't need him any more, he can go scratch his ass. He'll never get that duchy.

MAMA TURD. You're making a great mistake, Papa Turd. He'll turn against you.

PAPA TURD. Pooh! Too bad about him. I don't give any more of a damn for that little crumb than for Buggerlaus.

MAMA TURD. Hm, you think you've seen the last of Buggerlaus?

PAPA TURD. Blood and money! absolutely. What do you think he could do to me, that fourteen-year-old kid?

MAMA TURD. Papa Turd, mind what I'm telling you. You must try to win over Buggerlaus by your generosity.

PAPA TURD. What ! More money to hand out ? Once and
for all, no ! You already made me throw away more than
twenty-two million.

MAMA TURD. It's on your own head, Papa Turd. He'll cook
your goose.

PAPA TURD. Oh well, you'll be in the pot with me.

MAMA TURD. Listen to me, one last time. I am positive young
Buggerlaus will carry it off. After all, he thinks he has justice
on his side.

PAPA TURD. Oh, crap ! Isn't injustice just as good as justice ?
You annoy me, Mama Turd. I'm going to cut you to bits !

[MAMA TURD *runs away, pursued by* TURD.

[PAPA TURD, *alone.* – Hornstrumpot ! I'll start by grabbing
all the phynance. Then I'll kill everybody and leave. Here's
two that are dead already. Lucky there's a trapdoor to throw
them in. One ! Two ! The others will follow soon enough.]

SCENE II

The great hall of the palace.

PAPA TURD, MAMA TURD, OFFICERS *and* SOLDIERS ; GYRON, PILE,
    COCCYX ; NOBLES *in chains*, FINANCIERS, MAGISTRATES, HER-
    ALDS. [*In the cellar*, THE DEBRAINING MACHINE.

SUBTERRANEAN NOISES. *Kneading the glottises and larynges
of the jaw without a palate,*
    How fast the printer prints !
    The sequins tremble like the windmill's vanes,
    The leaves fall, in the teasing of the wind.
    The jaw of the skull without brains chews up the stranger's
brain,
        Sundays, on the hill, to the sound of fifes and drums,
        Or on red-letter days, in the endless cellars of the palace.
        Unfolding and explaining, the Debraining Machine,
        How fast, how fast, the printer prints !]

PAPA TURD. Bring in the crate of Nobles and the hook for Nobles and the sword for Nobles and the box of Nobles! And then – bring in the Nobles!

(*The* NOBLES *are brutally shoved in.*)

MAMA TURD. For heaven's sake, Papa Turd, restrain yourself.

PAPA TURD. I have the honor to inform you that for the enrichment of the realm I'm going to have the Nobles executed and seize all their property.

NOBLES. Horrors! Help, people and soldiers!

PAPA TURD. Bring in the first Noble, and pass me my Noble-hook. Those that are condemned to death I'll put through the trapdoor and they'll tumble into the sub-cellars of Pinchpork and Moneybag, where their brains will be removed by the printing-press. (*To the* NOBLE.) Who are you, stupid?

FIRST NOBLE. Count of Vitebsk.

PAPA TURD. What's your income?

FIRST NOBLE. Three million bagels.

PAPA TURD. Condemned! (*He grabs the* NOBLE *with the hook and puts him down the hole.*)

MAMA TURD. What vile ferocity!

PAPA TURD. Second Noble, who are you? (*The* NOBLE *says nothing.*) You going to answer, stupid?

SECOND NOBLE. G-G-G-Grand Duke of Posen.

PAPA TURD. Fine! fine! That's all I want to know. In the trap! – Third Noble, who are you? And what an ugly mug you've got.

THIRD NOBLE. Duke of Cortland and of the cities of Riga, Ravel, and Mitau.

PAPA TURD. Splendid! splendid! You haven't anything else?

THIRD NOBLE. Nothing.

PAPA TURD. Then, in the trap! – Fourth Noble, who are you?

FOURTH NOBLE. Prince of Podolia.

PAPA TURD. What's your income?

FOURTH NOBLE. I'm bankrupt.

PAPA TURD. For that dirty word, you go in the trap. – Fifth Noble, who are you ?

FIFTH NOBLE. Margrave of Thorn, Palatine of Polackia.

PAPA TURD. That's not much. Haven't you anything else ?

FIFTH NOBLE. It's enough for me.

PAPA TURD. Sure, better little than nothing. In the trap ! – What are you snivelling about, Mama Turd ?

MAMA TURD. You're so bloodthirsty, Papa Turd.

PAPA TURD. Bah, I'm getting rich. I think I'll have them read me MY list of MY properties. Herald, read me MY list of MY properties.

THE HERALD. Earldom of Sandomir . . .

PAPA TURD. Begin with the principalities, you stupid bugger !

THE HERALD. Principality of Podolia, Grand-Duchy of Posen, Duchy of Cortland, Earldom of Sandomir, Earldom of Vitebsk, Palatinate of Polackia, Margraviate of Thorn.

PAPA TURD. What else ?

THE HERALD. That's all.

PAPA TURD. Whaddya mean, that's all ? Oh, all right, let's get on with the Nobles. Seeing that it's taking so long to get rich, I'm going to have the whole bunch of them killed. That way I'll get all their vacant holdings. All right, throw the rest of the Nobles in the trap. (*The* NOBLES *are piled into the trap.*) Come on, hurry up. Now I want to make laws.

SEVERAL. That, we'll have to see.

PAPA TURD. First of all I'm going to reform justice, after which we'll proceed to the finances.

SEVERAL MAGISTRATES. We are opposed to any change whatsoever.

PAPA TURD. Pshit ! From now on, the magistrates don't get paid.

MAGISTRATES. And what will we live on ? We're poor.

PAPA TURD. You can have the fines you levy, and the property of whoever you condemn to death.

FIRST MAGISTRATE. Horrors!

SECOND. Infamy!

THIRD. Scandal!

FOURTH. Shame!

ALL. We refuse to judge under those circumstances.

PAPA TURD. In the trap with the magistrates!

(*They struggle in vain.*)

MAMA TURD. Oh my! What are you doing, Papa Turd? Who's to render justice now?

PAPA TURD. Me! You'll see how well things'll go.

MAMA TURD. Yes, that'll be just dandy.

PAPA TURD. Aw, shut up, big-mouth! – And now, gentlemen, we shall proceed to matters of finance.

FINANCIERS. There's nothing to change.

PAPA TURD. Whaddya mean? I want everything changed! First of all, I'm keeping half the taxes.

FINANCIERS. That's all?

PAPA TURD. Gentlemen, we'll put a ten percent tax on all property, another on commerce and industry, a third on marrying, a fourth [on not marrying, and a fifth] on dying – fifteen cents apiece.

FIRST FINANCIER. But that's idiotic, Papa Turd.

SECOND FINANCIER. It's absurd.

THIRD FINANCIER. It hasn't got head or tail.

PAPA TURD. Aha! you're trying to screw me. In the trap with the financiers! (*They stuff the* FINANCIERS *in.*)

MAMA TURD. But really, Papa Turd, what kind of a king are you? You're murdering everybody.

PAPA TURD. Ah, pshit!

MAMA TURD. No more justice, no more finance . . .

PAPA TURD. Fear nothing, my sweet child. I'll go from village to village myself, and collect the taxes. – [Pshit! In the trap! Bring in whoever's left of these eminent persons. (*Procession of notables of the moment, and text ad lib.*) You who so strangely resemble a well-known horseman in the park –

in the trap ! And you, Mr. Chief of Police, with all due re-
spect to you – in the trap ! In the trap with this English minister, and so as not to make anyone jealous, throw in a French
minister too – it doesn't matter who. And you, notable anti-
semite – in the trap ! And you, antisemitic Jew ; and you, rev-
erend priest ; and you, Mr. Apothecary ; and you, Mr. Cen-
sor ; and you, mister – in the trap ! Wait, here's a song-writer,
got in with the wrong key. We've had enough of him – in
the trap ! Oh, oh ! he isn't a song-writer, he's a story-writer
for the newspapers. What does it matter ? It's the same old
song. In the trap ! All right, everybody in the trap ! In the
trap ! In the trap ! Hurry up – in the trap ! In the trap ! In
the trap !]

[*Ad lib. from the translation credited to "Jane Warren &
Arnold Devree" (Judith Malina and Julian Beck) presented
at the Cherry Lane Theatre, New York, August 1952, with
Mungi Moskowitz as Ubu :*]

PAPA UBU. Oh, Shit ! Into the trap. And all the important
personages, into the trap . . . You, who look like a famous
critic for a highly respectable newspaper, into the trap. And
you, Chief of Police, into the trap ; and you, cop on the beat,
into the trap. Russian Delegate to the U.N., into the trap.
And to prove that we're not prejudiced, American Delegate
to the U.N. into the trap. Anybody and everybody into the
trap. Anti-Semites, into the trap. Semites, into the trap. Den-
tists, into the trap. Child actors, into the trap. Psychoanalysts,
psychoneurotics, psychopathics, and Fuller-brush-men, into
the trap. The whole world into the trap. Mayor Impellitteri,
into the trap. Winston Churchill, into the trap. Ernest Hem-
ingway, into the trap. Miss Rheingold, into the trap. Jean-
Louis Barrault, into the trap. e. e. cummings and Arthur
Godfrey, into the trap. Frank Lloyd Wright and Napoleon,
into the trap. Shirley Temple and Salvador Dali, into the
trap. Harry Truman, into the trap. Esther Williams, into the

trap. Mrs. George Washington Cavanaugh and Jean Cocteau, into the trap. General MacArthur, into the trap. Giselle, into the trap. Sister Kenny and Djuna Barnes, into the trap. Thomas Dewey and John Dewey and Admiral Dewey, into the trap. Brooks Atkinson, into the trap. Maxwell Bodenheim, into the trap. Eleanor Roosevelt and Louis Armstrong, into the trap. Perle Mesta, Pearl Bailey, Pearl Buck, into the trap. Mahatma Ghandi, into the trap. The waiters at Chumleys, into the trap. Pope Pius XII into the trap. Johnny Ray, into the trap. Jean Marais, into the trap. Adam and Eve and Rita Hayworth and Mohammed, into the trap. Gilbert and Sullivan, into the trap. Truman Capote and Tennessee Williams and Paul Bowles and Carson McCullers, into the trap. Cardinal Spellman, into the trap. Joe Gould, into the trap. Mary Martin and T. S. Eliot, into the trap. Cecil Beaton and Judge Medina, into the trap. Jesus Christ and Walter Chrysler, into the trap. Dean Martin and Jerry Lewis, into the trap. Merce Cunningham, into the trap. Ezra Pound and Maxwell Anderson, into the trap. Hamlet, into the trap. Reinhold Niebuhr, into the trap. The San Remo Cafe, into the trap. Helen Hayes and Ilse Koch, into the trap. Eugene O'Neill, into the trap. Dylan Thomas and Norman Thomas and Thomas Mann, into the trap. Greta Garbo, into the trap. Santa Claus and Santayana, into the trap. Dagmar, into the trap. Judy Garland, into the trap. Paul Goodman and Jane Russell, into the trap. Queen Juliana, Queen Elizabeth, the Queen of Spades, Butterfly McQueen and all the Queens, into the trap. Matisse and Bette Davis, into the trap. Gertrude Stein and Kirsten Flagstad, into the trap. Sigmund Rhee and Sigmund Freud, into the trap. Tallulah Bankhead and Wilhelm Reich, into the trap. Igor Stravinsky, into the trap. Milton Berle and Walter Winchell, into the trap. Martha Graham and Betty Grable, into the trap. Pablo Picasso and Clark Gable, into the trap. Hopalong Cassidy, Bernarr McFadden, Margaret O'Brien and Elsa Maxwell, into the trap. David Ben Gurion and George Balanchine, into the trap. Alfred Jarry, into the trap. (Myself – almost – into the trap.) Irving Berlin, into the trap. Anthony Eden and Li'l Abner and Pogo and J. Edgar Hoover, into the trap. Willie McGee, into the trap. Bing Crosby and W. H. Auden, into the trap. Al Capone, into the trap. Faustina, into the trap. Cecil B. De Mille, into the trap. John Ashbery, into the trap. Marshall Tito and Joe Palooka, into the trap. Billie Graham and Jimmy Durante, into the trap. Bonnie Prince Charlie and Francis Renault, into the trap. Sugar Ray Robinson and Lady Mendl, into the trap. Senator Kefauver, into the trap. Dr. Kinsey and Whistler's Mother, into the trap. Dorothy Thompson and Abraham Lincoln, into the trap. Charlie Chaplin and John the Baptist, into the trap. Judith Malina and Julian Beck, into the trap. Haile Selassie and Bertrand Russell, into the trap. The Trapp Family, into the trap. John Garfield, into the trap. Bernard Baruch, into the trap. Willie Sutton, into the trap. Paul Robeson and The Virgin Mary and Fleur Cowles, into the trap. Henry Luce and Marion Davies, into the trap. The D.A.R. and the Trappist Monks, into the trap. Rabbi Stephen S. Wise and Grandma Moses, into the trap. Sophie Tucker and John Cage, into the trap. Karen Horney and General Eisenhower, into the trap. Alfred Einstein and Eva Peron, into the trap. Robert Service, Civil Service, Diaper Service, and all the boys in the Service, *into the trap!*

SCENE III

A peasants' hovel on the outskirts of Warsaw.

Several PEASANTS *are assembled.*

A PEASANT (*coming in*). Did you hear the big news ? The king is dead, and the dukes too ; and Prince Buggerlaus got away to the mountains with his mother. And furthermore, Papa Turd has seized the throne.

ANOTHER. Yes, and here's something else. I just came from Cracow, and I saw them carting away the bodies of more than three hundred nobles and five hundred magistrates that they killed, and it seems they're going to double the taxes and Papa Turd is going to come and collect it in person.

ALL. God almighty! What will become of us? Papa Turd is a terrible swine, and they say his wife is horrible.

[*Tremendous knocking at the door.*]

A PEASANT. Listen! Wouldn't you say that someone is knocking at the door?

A VOICE (*outside*). Hornstrumpot! Open up! Now by my pshit, by Saint John, Saint Peter, and Saint Nicholas, open up! Blood and money! Hornducats! I've come for the taxes!

(*The door is stove in.* TURD *comes through the hole, followed by his troop of penny-pinchers.*)

SCENE IV

PAPA TURD. Which one of you is the oldest? (A PEASANT *steps forward.*) What's your name?

THE PEASANT. Stanislas Leczinski.

PAPA TURD. Well then, hornstrumpot, listen carefully or these gentlemen will cut off your years. So are you going to listen to me?

STANISLAS. But Your Excellency hasn't said anything yet.

PAPA TURD. Whaddya mean! I've been talking for an hour. Do you think I came here to preach to the wilderness?

STANISLAS. Such a thought is the farthest from my mind.

PAPA TURD. Now then, I've come to tell you and direct you and inform you that you have to produce and show your cash immediately, or you'll be massacred. Hey there, noble snot-noses of Phynance, trundle in the honey-wagon. (*They bring in the wagon.*)

STANISLAS. Sire, we are down on the register for only one hundred and fifty-two bagels, which we've already paid six weeks ago come Michaelmas.

PAPA TURD. That's very possible, but I've changed the government and I've had it announced in the newspapers that all the taxes have to be paid twice, and three times those that will be designated later. With this system I'll make my fortune in a hurry; then I'll kill everybody and leave.

PEASANTS. Mercy, Master Turd! Have pity on us. We're just poor people.

PAPA TURD. Frig that. Pay.

PEASANTS. But we can't. We *have* paid.

PAPA TURD. Pay! Or I'll have to discipline you with torture and uncoupling of the neck from the head! Hornstrumpot, I am the king, surely?

ALL. Oh, so that's how it is! To arms! Up with Buggerlaus, by the grace of God King of Poland and Lithuania!

PAPA TURD. Forward, gentlemen of Phynance! Do your duty. (*A fight ensues. The house is destroyed, and old* STANISLAS *flees alone across the plains.* TURD *stays behind to pick up the money.*)

SCENE V

A dungeon in the fortress of Thorn.

BORDURE *in chains*, PAPA TURD

PAPA TURD. Ah, citizen, that's how it is. You wanted me to pay you what I owed you, and when I wouldn't you revolted. You plotted against me, and here you are – in the trap. Hornducats ! Not bad, eh ? The trick is so neatly turned you ought to find it very much to your taste.

BORDURE. Take care, Papa Turd. In the five days you've been king, you've committed more crimes than it would take to damn all the saints in Paradise. The blood of a king and of his nobles cry vengeance, and their cries will be heard.

PAPA TURD. Eh, my dear friend, you've got a well-oiled tongue ! I don't doubt that if you should escape, complications might set in, but I don't believe the dungeons of Thorn have ever given up any of the fine young men entrusted to them. And so, good night, sleep tight, and keep your legs crossed, because the rats here dance a very pretty sarabande. [*He goes.*

(*The turnkeys come and bolt all the doors.*)

SCENE VI

The palace at Moscow.

THE EMPEROR ALEXIS *and his court*, BORDURE

CZAR ALEXIS. Was it you, infamous adventurer, who helped to murder our cousin Wenceslaus ?

BORDURE. Sire, forgive me. I was dragged into it in spite of myself by Papa Turd.

ALEXIS. What a liar ! Anyway, what do you want ?

BORDURE. Papa Turd pretended I was conspiring against him, and threw me in prison. I succeeded in escaping, and spurred my horse five days and nights across the steppes to come and beg your gracious mercy.

ALEXIS. What do you bring as a token of your submission?

BORDURE. My free sword and a detailed plan of the fortress of Thorn.

ALEXIS. I accept the sword, but by Saint George, burn the plan! I don't want to owe my victory to treachery.

BORDURE. One of Wenceslaus' sons, Prince Buggerlaus, escaped alive. I'll do anything to restore him to the throne.

ALEXIS. What rank did you hold in the Polish army?

BORDURE. Captain of the 5th regiment of Wilnauer dragoons and of a company of mercenaries in the pay of Papa Turd.

ALEXIS. Good. I appoint you second-lieutenant in the 10th Cossack regiment, and beware if you turn traitor! But fight well, and you shall be rewarded.

BORDURE. It's not courage I lack, Sire.

ALEXIS. That is well. Disappear from my presence.

[*He goes.*

SCENE VII

TURD'S *council-chamber.*

PAPA TURD, MAMA TURD, COUNCILLORS OF PHYNANCE

PAPA TURD. Gentlemen, the meeting is now open. Try to listen carefully and keep calm. First we're going to deal with the subject of phynances. After that we'll talk about a little system I've invented for bringing good weather and conjuring rain.

A COUNCILLOR. Very good indeed, Master Turd.

MAMA TURD. What a blockhead!

PAPA TURD. Madam of my pshit, take care. I won't put up with any more of your nonsense. – Well then, gentlemen, I will inform you that the phynances are going fairly well. Every morning a considerable number of dogs in woollen stockings pour into the streets, and the dognappers are doing fine. On all sides one can see burning houses, and people bending under the weight of our phynance.

THE COUNCILLOR. And the new taxes, Master Turd, how are they going?

MAMA TURD. Not at all. The tax on marriage hasn't brought in more than eleven cents, and Papa Turd is chasing people all over the place to make them get married.

PAPA TURD. Blood and money! Horn of my strumpot! Madam financier, haven't I years to speak with and you a mouth to hear me? (*Burst of laughter.*) Or rather, no! You're the one that's making me make mistakes! You're to blame for my stupidity! Now turdhorn!... (A MESSENGER *enters.*) Now what does he want? Beat it, louse, or I'll fix you good with beheading and with twisting of the legs.

[MESSENGER *leaves.*

MAMA TURD. There! he's gone now, but he dropped a letter.

PAPA TURD. You read it. Either I'm losing my mind, or else I don't know how to read. Hurry up, buggerlet, this ought to be from Bordure.

MAMA TURD. Precisely. He says the Czar received him very well, that he's going to invade your dominions and re-establish Buggerlaus, and that you will be killed.

PAPA TURD. Hoo! Hah! I'm scared! Ooh, I'm scared! I'm at death's door. Oh, poor man that I am. What's to become of me, God in heaven? This wicked man is going to kill me. Saint Anthony and all the rest of the saints, protect me! I'll pay cash. I'll even burn candles to you. God almighty, what's to be done? (*He weeps and sobs.*)

MAMA TURD. There's only one way out, Papa Turd.

PAPA TURD. What's that, my love?

MAMA TURD. War!!

ALL. Praise God! That's the honorable thing to do!

PAPA TURD. Oh sure, that way I'll get beaten even worse.

FIRST COUNCILLOR. Come on! Let's go and mobilize the army...

SECOND. And assemble the provisions...

THIRD. And prepare the artillery and the fortifications...

FOURTH. And raise the money to pay the troops.

PAPA TURD. No, by Jesus! I'll kill you, you . . . ! I won't hand out any money. And that's another thing – before I was paid to make war. Now I have to do it at my own expense. No, by my green candle! Since you're all so set on it, by all means let's have war, but don't let's pay out a cent.

ALL. Hurray for war!

SCENE VIII

The encampment before Warsaw.
[At right, a mill with a usable window.
At left, rocks. Backdrop showing the ocean.

THE POLISH ARMY (*one soldier*) enters, led by GENERAL LASKY

SONG OF THE ARMY

My tunic has two, three, four buttons,
Five buttons!
Six, seven, eight buttons,
Nine buttons!
Ten, 'leven, twelve buttons,
Thirteen buttons!
My tunic has thirteen, fourteen, fifteen buttons,
Sixteen buttons!
Eighteen, nineteen, twenty buttons,
Twenty buttons!
Twenty-one, two, three buttons,
Thirty buttons!
My tunic has thirty buttons, forty buttons,
. . . ty buttons!
Forty-three, four, five buttons,
five buttons!
Sixty-eight, nine, ten buttons.
ten buttons!
My tunic has fifty million buttons,
million buttons . . .

GENERAL LASKY. Company . . . halt! Left . . . face!
Front! Right . . . dress! Eyes front. At ease. Men, this stuff
some sources sling about Poland wanting to stay out of war,
and not wanting to fight, is a crock of pshit! Polanders *love*
to fight. Never forget that. You're military men, and military
men make the best soldiers. So to do sentry-duty honorably
and victoriously, rest the weight of your body on your right
foot, and start off rapidly with your left. 'Ten-tion! Left
by the left flank . . . pshit! Company . . . forward . . .
guide right . . . march! One two, one two . . .

THE ARMY, *with* LASKY *at its flank, marches off cheering :*]

SOLDIERS *and* CHAMPIONS. Hurray for Poland! Hurray for
Papa Turd!

PAPA TURD [*entering with casque and cuirass*]. Hey, Mama
Turd, hand me down my swagger-stick and breast-plate.
Pretty soon I'm going to be so loaded down I won't be able to
run if they chase me.

MAMA TURD. Pfui, what a coward!

PAPA TURD. Hey! my pshit-sword is running away and the
money-crook is uncrooking! All this junk is getting in my
way. I'll never be ready, and the Russians are advancing and
want to kill me.

A SOLDIER. Master Turd, you're losing your yard-scissors.

PAPA TURD. I'm gonna kill ya with my pshit-hook and mug-
knife.

MAMA TURD. Oh my, how handsome he looks with his hel-
met and breast-plate. You'd think he was an armed pumpkin.

PAPA TURD. [Our Champions are also of great importance,
but not nearly as handsome as when I was King of Aragon.
Like skinned things, or a diagram of the circulation of the
venous and arterial blood, the financial bile oozed out of them
through holes, and crept in through fistulas of gold and
copper. They were numbered too, and I led them in battle
with a halter from which hung funeral leads. How happily
the women aborted before them, because the babies would be

born like them. – And the coprophagous porkers vomited in
horror.] And now I'm going to get on my horse. Gentlemen,
bring on the money-go-mare.

MAMA TURD. Papa Turd, your horse won't be able to carry
you. It hasn't eaten anything for five days, and it's nearly dead.

PAPA TURD. How do you like that! They're making me
pay a dime a day for this nag, and she can't carry me. Turdhorn! Either you're kidding me or you're robbing me. (MAMA
TURD blushes, and lowers her eyes.) All right, get me another
beast, but I won't go on foot. Hornstrumpot! (CHAMPION
GYRON [in blackface] leads in an enormous horse.) Thank you,
faithful Gyron. (He pats the horse.) Ho, ho . . . Now I'm
getting on. Oh! I better sit down. I'm falling off! (The horse
starts.) Help! Stop the horse! God almighty, I'm liable to
fall off and get killed!!!

(He disappears into the wings.)

MAMA TURD. What an imbecile. (She laughs.) Oh, he's up
again! No, he's down.

PAPA TURD (re-entering on horseback). Fizzihorn! I'm half
dead. But it doesn't matter. It's war! I'm going to war, and
I'll kill everybody. Anybody steps out of line – watch out! I'll
fix 'im with twisting of the nose and teeth, and extraction of
the tongue.

MAMA TURD. Good luck, Mr. Turd!

PAPA TURD. I forgot to tell you. I'm making you regent. But
I'm taking the account-book with me, and God help you if
you rob me. And I'm leaving Champion Gyron to help you.
Farewell, Mama Turd. [Let huswifery appear; keep close thy
buggle-boe.]

MAMA TURD. Goodbye, Papa Turd. Kill the Czar good.

PAPA TURD. Positively. Twisting of the nose and teeth, extraction of the tongue, insertion of the little swagger stick in
the years.

(Fanfare. The army marches off.)

SCENE IX

MAMA TURD, CHAMPION GYRON

MAMA TURD (*alone*). Now that this overgrown puppet is gone, we can get down to business : to kill Buggerlaus and seize all the treasures of Poland. [Here, Gyron, come and help me.

CHAMPION GYRON. To do what, Mistress ?

MAMA TURD. Everything ! My husband wants you to take his place while he's at war. So tonight . . .

CHAMPION GYRON. Oh, Mistress !

MAMA TURD. Don't blush, my dear. In the first place, on you it's invisible. But before anything else, give me a hand carting away these treasures.

(*Patter song, spoken very quickly as they carry the treasures off:*)

MAMA TURD (*picking up a chamber-pot*)

Now first to my astonished eyes,
The pole, the pole, the Polish prize !

CHAMPION GYRON

In this reindeer skin she got out of bed,
The poor dear queen who now is dead !

MAMA TURD

The spitting image, top to toe,
Of my missing spouse that I love so.

CHAMPION GYRON

Oh the empty bottles, we say and sing,
And the good old days of the Bastard King.

MAMA TURD (*picking up a clysterpump*)

Oh the winding, twining old hookah
That they built for Queen Marie Leczinska.

CHAMPION GYRON

The papers hidden in a pumpkin head
To defend the state from the dirty Red.

MAMA TURD (*picking up a little broom*)

And the whisk-broom used by the Queen's Navee
To help Great Poland sweep the sea.

MAMA TURD. Aiee ! I hear a noise ! Papa Turd is coming
back ! So soon ?! Quick, run !
                    They run away, letting the treasures fall.]

ACT IV

SCENE I

*The crypt of the ancient kings of Poland
in the cathedral of Warsaw.*

MAMA TURD, *alone*

MAMA TURD. Now, where is this treasure? Not a single stone rings hollow. All the same, I did count thirteen flagstones from the tomb of Ladislaus the Great going along the wall, and there's nothing here. Someone must have deceived me. No, here it is! This stone rings hollow. To work, Mama Turd! That's it, we'll unbed this stone. It holds fast. We'll use the end of the money-crook – it will serve its purpose this time. There! There's the gold in the midst of the bones of kings. Into the bag, now, all of it! Oh! what was that noise? In these old vaults, can anything still live? No, it's nothing. Hurry now. Take everything. This gold will be better off in daylight than among the graves of bygone princes. Put back the stone. Now what? – again that noise! This place gives me the horrors. I'll get the rest of the gold some other time – I'll come back tomorrow.

A VOICE (*rising from the tomb of* JAN SIGISMUND). Never, Mama Turd!

> (MAMA TURD *runs away terrified, carrying off
> the stolen gold through a secret door.*)

SCENE II

The town square in Warsaw.

BUGGERLAUS *and his partisans*, PEOPLE *and* SOLDIERS

BUGGERLAUS. Forward, my friends ! Long live Wenceslaus and Poland ! That old blackguard, Papa Turd, is gone. No one is left but the old witch, Mama Turd, and her knight. I offer to march at your head, and re-establish the race of my forefathers.

ALL. Hurrah for Buggerlaus !

BUGGERLAUS. And I'll revoke all the taxes established by that terrible Papa Turd.

ALL. Hooray !! Let's go. We'll rush the palace, and wipe out the whole brood.

BUGGERLAUS. Aha ! Here comes Mama Turd down the palace steps with her guards.

MAMA TURD. What is it you want, gentlemen ? – Oh !! it's Buggerlaus ! (*The crowd starts throwing stones.*)

FIRST GUARD. All the windows are broken.

SECOND GUARD. Holy Saint George, they got me !

THIRD GUARD. Holy Moses, I'm dying !

BUGGERLAUS. Keep throwing stones, my friends !

CHAMPION GYRON. Hey ! So that's how it is ! (*He unsheathes his sword and rushes in, wreaking terrible carnage.*)

BUGGERLAUS. Have at you ! On guard, cowardly bumpkin !

(*They fight.*)

CHAMPION GYRON. I'm done for !

BUGGERLAUS. Victory, my friends ! And now for Mama Turd ! (*Trumpets are heard.*) Great ! Here come the Nobles. Hurry, seize the evil harpy !

THE OTHERS. Yes, until we can throttle the old bandit himself !

(MAMA TURD *runs away, followed by all the Poles.*
Shots, and showers of stones.)

SCENE III

*The Polish army on the march
in the Ukraine.*

PAPA TURD [*enters dragging a long bridle*]. Blasthole! leg-o'-god! sowbelly! We're perishing. We're dying of thirst and tiredness. Honorable Soldier, have the kindness to carry our phynance-box, and you, Honorable Lancer, take charge of the pshit-shears and physic-stick to lighten our person, because, I repeat, we're dying of fatigue. (*The soldiers obey.*)

PILE. Hey! Mister! It's funny the Russians don't show up.

PAPA TURD. It is regrettable that the state of our phynance doesn't permit us to have transportation to match our size; because, for fear of demolishing our nag, we've come the whole way on foot, dragging (*the horse now appears*) our horse by the bridle. But when we get back to Poland, we will invent by means of our knowledge of pataphysics, and aided by the enlightenment of our councillors, [an automobile to carry our horse, and] an aeroplane to transport the whole army.

COCCYX. Here comes Nicholas Rensky all of a rush.

PAPA TURD. What's bothering that guy?

RENSKY. All is lost, Sire! The Poles have rebelled, Gyron [has disappeared] and Mama Turd has fled to the mountains taking with her all the treasures and phynance of the realm.

PAPA TURD. Already!!! Bird of night, beast of misfortune, owl in gaiters! Where did you dredge up this nonsense? Oh well, from bad to worse. And who did it? Buggerlaus, I bet. Where are you coming from?

RENSKY. From Warsaw, noble Sire.

PAPA TURD. Boy of my pshit, if I believed you I'd make the whole army retrace its steps. But, honored youth, there's more feathers than brains in your head. You've dreamt foolishness. Back to the front, my boy. The Russians aren't too far off, and soon we'll have to attack with everything we've got – pshit, physic, and phynance.

GENERAL LASKY. Papa Turd, wouldn't you say you see the Russians on the plain ?

PAPA TURD. My god, the Russians ! That does it ! If I thought I could still get away – but no, we're on a height and exposed on all sides.

THE ARMY. The Russians ! The enemy !

PAPA TURD. Come, gentlemen, let us take our positions for the battle. We're going to stay on this hill and never commit the stupidity of coming down off it. I'll stay in the middle like a living citadel, and the rest of you will gravitate around me. I must beg of you to cram your muskets with as many balls as they'll hold, because 8 balls can kill 8 Russians and that's just so many more I won't have on my back. We'll put the infantry at the bottom of the hill to receive the Russians and kill them a little, the cavalry behind to throw themselves into the confusion, and the artillery around the windmill here to fire into the heap. As for us, we'll stay inside the windmill and fire through the window with our phynance-pistol. Across the door we'll put our physic-stick, and anyone who tries to get in – watch out for the pshit-hook !

OFFICERS. Your orders, Sir Turd, shall be obeyed.

PAPA TURD. Fine. Everything is taken care of. We're going to win. What time is it ? [*Sound-effect:* Cuckoo ! *three times.*]

GENERAL LASKY. Eleven o'clock.

PAPA TURD. All right, let's go to lunch. The Russians won't attack before noon. Honorable General, tell the soldiers to take a fast crap and intone the Phynance Song.

SOLDIERS *and* CHAMPIONS

God save our Papa Turd,
Our gracious Phynancier
Bing, bing, bing, bing.
Bing, bing, bing, bing.
Bing, bing – bazink !

[LASKY. 'Ten-tion ! Right face – left face. Form a circle. Two steps forward . . . Hump ! (THE ARMY *marches out.*

Trumpet flourish. PAPA TURD *begins to sing,* THE ARMY *coming back for the Chorus at the end of the first stanza.*)

CHANSON POLONAISE

PAPA TURD :   Now when I sip
                My little brown jug,
                It's down the hatch
                With a glug glug glug !

Chorus :   Glug glug glug, glug glug glug.

PAPA TURD :   When thirst pursues,
                To drink we flee,
                If you can't get a bottle
                Use an old képi !

Chorus :   Pee pee pee, pee pee pee.

PAPA TURD :   Now by my moustache,
                Don't you dare say Bah !
                To the proud white plume
                On my old tchapska !

Chorus :   Ca ca ca, ca ca ca.

PAPA TURD :   Your nose gets pimpled
                And your strumpot too,
                So drink to Poland
                And to Père Ubu !

Chorus :   Poo poo poo, poo poo poo.

PAPA TURD. Oh, the fine fellows, I love them ! And now, let's eat !

THE SOLDIERS. To the attack !

PAPA TURD (*watching them go*). Tell Mr. Honorable Kitchen Police to bring on the victuals held in reserve for the entire army.

LASKY. But Papa Turd, there aren't any victuals – there's nothing to eat.

PAPA TURD. You swine! whaddya mean there's nothing to eat? What can our military commissariat be thinking of?

LASKY. Don't you remember? You threw them all in the trap.

PAPA TURD. Oh yes! Now I can breathe freely. I knew this excellent administration couldn't possibly make such a mistake. Everybody knows it loves to stuff the troops with trumps – I mean rumps of turkey, roast chicken, dog-paste, cauliflower à la pshit, and other fowl. But still I'll have to see if there's anything left to line my belly with . . . because *I'm* hungry. (*Cannonade begins offstage.*) Now what am I going to put in my strumpot?] (*A Russian cannonball arrives, breaks off one vane of the mill and hits him in the belly.*) Hoo! Hah! I'm hit! God almighty, I'm dead! And yet, no – I'm all right.

SCENE IV

THE SAME, A CAPTAIN, *then* THE RUSSIAN ARMY

A CAPTAIN (*coming in*). Master Turd, the Russians are attacking.

PAPA TURD. So what? What do you expect me to do about it? I didn't tell them to. However, gentlemen of Phynance, let's get ready for the fray. (*A second cannonball.* PAPA TURD *is bowled over, the cannonball bouncing up and down on his strumpot several times before coming to a stop.*)

GENERAL LASKY. A second cannonball! [I'm getting out of here. – *He flees.*]

PAPA TURD. I've had enough. It's raining lead and iron here. Our precious person might even get damaged. – Hey you, Russian soldiers! Be careful! Don't shoot this way; there's somebody here! – Let's get going.

(*They all go down the hill on the run. The battle has just begun. They disappear into torrents of smoke at the foot of the hill.*)

A RUSSIAN (*striking*). For God and the Czar!

RENSKY. I'm dead!

PAPA TURD. Forward!! Listen, mister, you that I'm hitting because you tried to hit me first – do you understand, you drunken bum, with your musket that doesn't go off?!

THE RUSSIAN. Is that so? (*He shoots him with a revolver.*)

PAPA TURD. Ah! Ooh! I'm wounded! I'm riddled! I'm perforated! I'm done for! I'm buried! No, wait – he missed me! There!! I got him! (*He rips him open.*) Now start something!

GENERAL LASKY. Forward! Skip the ditch! Let's go! Victory is ours!!

PAPA TURD. You think so? So far I got a lot more lumps on my head than laurels.

RUSSIAN CAVALRY [*in the wings*]. Huzza!! Make way for the Czar!

(THE CZAR *enters, accompanied by* BORDURE *in disguise.*)

A POLE. Oh, Christ! Every man for himself! Here comes the Czar!

ANOTHER. My God! He's crossing the moat.

A THIRD. Biff! Bam! There's four done in by that big bugger of a lieutenant.

BORDURE. All right, had enough, you bastards?! There, Jan Sobiesky, that'll fix you! (*He kills him.*) Now for the rest!

(*He massacres the Poles.*)

PAPA TURD. Forward, my friends! Get that son of a bitch! We'll smear the Muscovites! Victory is ours! Hurray for the Double Eagle!

ALL. Forward! Leg-o'-god! Get the big bugger!

BORDURE. By Saint George, they got me.

PAPA TURD (*recognizing him*). It's you, Bordure! Ah, my friend, we are delighted, along with everyone else present, to see you again. I'm going to cook you over a slow fire! Gentlemen of Phynance, light a fire. – Oh! Ooh! I'm dead. I must've been hit by a cannonball at least. Oh God, forgive all my sins. Yes, it must have been a cannonball.

BORDURE. You've been shot with a cap-pistol.

PAPA TURD. Aha! you're making fun of me! Again? I'll fix you! (*He throws himself on* BORDURE *and rips him apart.*)

GENERAL LASKY. Papa Turd, we're advancing on all fronts.

PAPA TURD. So I see. I'm all worn out. I'm half kicked to death, and I've got to sit down. [*Sits on the ground.*] Ouch! my bottle!

GENERAL LASKY. Get the Czar's instead, Papa Turd.

PAPA TURD. Eh? That's just what I'm going to do. Here I go! Pshit-sword, do your duty, and you, money-crook, don't fall behind. Physic-stick, imitate them unstintingly, and share with this little tip of wood the honor of massacring, goosing, and giving the business to the Muscovite Czar. Forward, Mr. Money-go-mare! (*He throws himself on* THE CZAR.)

[THE CZAR. Choknozoff, catastrophe, crapazoff !]

PAPA TURD. Take that, you ! (THE CZAR *snatches the stick away from* PAPA TURD *and hits him with it.*) Oh ! Ouch ! Gee whiz ! I'm licked ! I take it all back, Sir ! I didn't do it on purpose ! (*He runs away,* THE CZAR *chasing him.*) Holy Virgin, this lunatic is chasing me ! God almighty, what have I done ? Oh, good ! there's still the moat to cross. Help ! he's right behind me, and the moat in front ! Courage ! I'll just shut my eyes. (*He leaps over the ditch.* THE CZAR *falls in.*)

THE CZAR. Shucks ! I'm stuck.

POLES. Hurray ! the Czar is down !

PAPA TURD. I don't dare look back ! Hey, he's stuck in the ditch, and they're hitting him on the head. That's it, Poles, hit him again ! He's got a broad back, the son of a bitch ! Just the same, our prediction was completely realized : the physic-stick did marvels, and there isn't a doubt in the world that I'd have finished him off myself if an inexplicable terror hadn't overpowered and annulled in ourself the effects of our courage. But we were suddenly obliged to turn tail, and owe our preservation only to our dexterity as a horseman and likewise to the solidity of the hocks of our money-go-mare, whose speed is equalled only by its strength, and whose agility is celebrated in song and story, and likewise to the great depth of the ditch which lay so opportunely in the path of the enemy of ourself, yours truly, Master of Phynance. All of which is very pretty, but no one is listening. Hey, look ! Here we go again ! (*The Russian dragoons charge, and rescue* THE CZAR.)

GENERAL LASKY (*running across*). This time it's a rout !

PAPA TURD. Aha ! Then it's time to get out of here. There-fore, gentlemen of Poland, forward ! – or rather, backward !

POLES. Every man for himself !

PAPA TURD. Come on, let's go ! What a mob, what a rout, what a multitude ! How am I going to get out of this mess ? (*He is knocked over.*) Listen, you ! Watch what you're doing, or you're going to experience the fiery courage of the Master of Phynance. There, he's gone. Now we can run away, and in a hurry too, while Lasky isn't looking. (*He runs off*. THE CZAR *and the Russian army are seen pursuing the Poles*.)

[PAPA TURD, *coming back*. – Nobody here ? What a mob, what a rout ! God almighty, where can I hide ? Ah, in this little house. I'll surely be safe here.

LASKY (*sticking his head out of the mill*). Who's there ?

PAPA TURD. Help ! Oh, it's you, Lasky. You here too ? Didn't you get killed yet ? . . . I can't go on. Suddenly I have a strange need to sleep. But I can't sleep here, because even with a cotton nightcap (*pulling one on*) I'm still afraid of drafts. And you know the old saying : anyone that's afraid of drafts shouldn't sleep in a windmill.]

SCENE V

A cavern in Lithuania.
It is snowing.

PAPA TURD, PILE, COCCYX

PAPA TURD. What awful weather ! It's freezing hard enough to split rocks, and the person of the Master of Phynance is suffering terribly.

PILE. Hey ! Mister Turd, did you get over your terror and your flight ?

PAPA TURD. Yes, I'm not scared any more, but I'm still running.

COCCYX (*aside*). What a pig !

PAPA TURD. Hmm. Master Coccyx, your yard, how does it feel ?

COCCYX. As well as it can, Mister. It could feel worse. In consequeynt of the fact thatte the lead in my pants bends it to the ground, and I haven't been able to extract the ball.

PAPA TURD. Well, that's fine. And you were always such a great one for hitting other people. Me, I displayed the greatest courage. Without endangering myself in the least, I massacred four of the enemy with my bare hands, not counting those that were already dead when I dispatched them.

COCCYX. Pile, do y'know what became of little Rensky?

PILE. He got a bullet through the head.

PAPA TURD. Ah yes, just as the corn-poppy and the pissabed are mowed down in the flower of their youth by the merciless mow of the merciless mower who mows mercilessly their pitiful phizz, just so did little Rensky play the corn-poppy. Valiantly did he fight, but all the same – there were too many Russians.

PILE *and* COCCYX. Hey! Mister!

AN ECHO [*in the wings*]. Harumph!

PILE. What's that grunting? Let's arm ourselves with the torches.

PAPA TURD. Oh God, no! More Russians, I bet! I've had enough! If they annoy me I'm gonna fuggem good, and that's all there is to it.

SCENE VI

Enter A BEAR

COCCYX. Hey! Mister Phynance!

PAPA TURD. Oh, my! See the little bow-wow. Isn't he nice.

PILE. Look out! Ow, what an enormous bear! My cartridges!

PAPA TURD. A bear? Oh, the monstrous beast! Poor poor me, I'm eaten alive! God save me! He's coming for me! No, it's Coccyx he's after. Oh! I can breathe again. (THE BEAR *throws himself on* COCCYX. PILE *slashes at him with a knife.* PAPA TURD *takes refuge on a high rock.*)

COCCYX. Help, Pile! Help! Save me, Mister Turd!

PAPA TURD. Nothing doing! Get out of it the best you can, my friend. At the moment we're saying our Pater Noster. Everybody'll have his turn to get eaten.

PILE. I got him ! I'm holding him !

COCCYX. Hold tight, my friend. He's beginning to let go of me.

PAPA TURD. Hallowèd be Thy name . . .

COCCYX. Cowardly bugger !

PILE. Ow ! He's biting me ! Oh God, save me, I'm dying.

PAPA TURD. Thy will be done . . .

COCCYX. Ah ! I've wounded him !

PILE. Hurray ! he's losing blood ! (THE BEAR *bellows in pain amidst the shouts of the two* CHAMPIONS. PAPA TURD *continues to mutter*.)

COCCYX. Hold him tight while I get in my dynamite punch.

PAPA TURD. Give us this day our daily bread . . .

PILE. Hurry up, I can't hold on much longer.

PAPA TURD. As we forgive those who trespass against us . . .

COCCYX. I got it !! (*Tremendous explosion.* THE BEAR *falls dead*.)

PILE *and* COCCYX. Victory !!

PAPA TURD. But deliver us from evil, Amen. All right, is he dead yet ? Can I get down off the rock ?

PILE (*disgustedly*). Just as you like.

PAPA TURD (*coming down*). There ! You see – he's dead ; and here we are, perfectly all right. You may flatter yourselves that if you are still living, still trampling the snows of Lithuania, you owe it to the magnanimous virtue, courage, and presence of mind of the Master of Phynance, who strained himself, broke his back, and practically got a sore throat saying paternosters for your safety, and who wielded the spiritual sword of prayer with as much courage as you handled the temporal dynamite-punch of the here-present Champion Coccyx. We have taken our devotion even further, in that we did not hesitate to climb upon a mighty rock so that our prayers might have less far to go to get to heaven.

PILE. Revolting she-ass !

PAPA TURD. Well well, what a big beast. Thanks to me, you now have something to eat. What a belly, gentlemen ! The Greeks would have been more comfortable in there than in their wooden horse, and we were very near, dear friends, to being able to verify with our own eyes his internal capacity.

PILE. I'm starving. What is there to eat?

COCCYX. The bear!

PAPA TURD. Eh, poor lads, are you going to eat him raw? We haven't anything to start a fire with.

PILE. Haven't we got our musket-flints?

PAPA TURD. Hmm, that's right. And besides, I think I see over there, not too far away, a little woods where there ought to be some dry branches. Go and get some, Master Coccyx.

(COCCYX *goes off across the snow.*)

PILE. And now, Master Turd, go ahead and carve up the bear.

PAPA TURD. Oh no! Maybe he isn't quite dead yet. Whereas you, who are already half eaten, and bitten all over, you're just made for the part. I'll light a fire while we're waiting for the wood. (PILE *begins to carve up the bear.*) Oh! Watch out! He moved.

PILE. But Master Turd, he's already cold.

PAPA TURD. That's too bad. It would have been better for the system to eat him hot. This is going to give the Master of Phynance indigestion.

PILE (*aside*). Isn't he disgusting? (*Aloud.*) Give us a hand, Mr. Turd, I can't do the whole job myself.

PAPA TURD. No, I don't feel like doing anything. I'm very tired, as a matter of fact.

COCCYX (*returning*). What snow, my friends! You'd think you were in Sunny Spain or at the North Pole. But it's beginning to get dark. Inside of an hour it will be night. Let's hurry while we still can see.

PAPA TURD. Yes, you hear that, Pile? Hurry up! Both of you, hurry up. Put the beast on a spit and cook 'im. I'm hungry.

PILE. That's the last straw! Listen, pig, you work or you don't eat. Understand?

PAPA TURD. Oh well, it's all the same to me. I'd just as soon eat it raw, you know. It's you who'll suffer. Anyhow, I'm sleepy.

COCCYX. What'll we do, Pile? Let's eat it all ourselves. He don't get any. Or else we could give him the bones.

PILE. Fine. There! the fire is catching.

PAPA TURD. Oh! that's nice. It's warm now. But I see Russians everywhere. God almighty, what a rout! Oh! (*He falls asleep.*)

COCCYX. I wonder if what Rensky said is true – if Mama Turd really was dethroned. It wouldn't be a bit impossible.

PILE. Let's finish eating.

COCCYX. No, we have more important things to do. I think it would be a good idea for us to look into the truth of this rumor.

PILE. You're right. Ought we to abandon Papa Turd, or stay here with him?

COCCYX. The night brings counsel. Let's go to sleep. To-morrow we'll decide what ought to be done.

PILE. No, better to profit by the darkness and get away.

COCCYX. Well then, let's go.   [*They leave.*

SCENE VII

[*Nightmare, with apparition of rats, spiders, etc., the Guignol classic.*]

TURD (*talking in his sleep*). Hey you, Russian soldiers! Be careful! Don't shoot this way; there's somebody here! Oh! there's Bordure. He's a bad one – you'd think he was a bear. And Buggerlaus, coming at me! The bear, the bear! Oh, he's down! Great God, how tough he is! Me, I don't want to do any work. Be off with you, Buggerlaus! Do you hear me, you fool? There's Rensky now, and the Czar! Oh! they're going to hit me. And Madame Turde! Where'd you get all that gold ? You've stolen my gold, you wretch ! You've been rummaging in my tomb in the Warsaw Cathedral, near the Moon. I've been dead a long time. It was Buggerlaus that killed me, and I'm buried at Warsaw with Wladislaus the Great, and also at Cracow with Jan Sigismund, and also at Thorn in the dungeon with Bordure. There he is again ! Be off with you, accursed bear – you look just like Bordure ! Do you hear me, you imp of Satan ? No, he can't hear. The Snot-noses have cut off his years. That's it ! Off with their heads ! Murdder 'em ! Chop yards ! Pinch pennies ! And drink yourself to death ! That's the life of a Snot-nose – that's the luck of a Master of Phynance. (*He falls silent and sleeps.*)

ACT V

SCENE I

It is night. PAPA TURD *is sleeping.*

MAMA TURD *enters without seeing him.*
It is pitch dark.

MAMA TURD. At last I find shelter. Here I shall be alone. No harm done, but what a headlong flight – to cross the whole of Poland in four days! Every possible misfortune assailed me at once. No sooner does that great fat clown leave, but I go to the crypt to get the treasure. Right afterwards I almost get stoned to death by Buggerlaus and his madmen. I lose my cavalier, Champion Gyron, who was so enamored of my charms that he used to swoon with delight every time he looked at me, and even, I was told, when he didn't look at me – which is the height of passion. Poor boy, he would have let himself be cut in half for me, and the proof is, he was cut into quarters by Buggerlaus. Biff, bam, boom! I thought I'd die. Then, afterwards, I take flight, followed by the furious mob. I leave the palace. I come to the Vistula. All the bridges were guarded. I swim across, hoping to tire my pursuers. From all sides the nobility assembled to chase me. A thousand times I escaped being killed, half smothered by a mob of Polacks lusting for my blood. In the end I escaped their fury, and after four days of racing through the snows of what was my kingdom, I arrive and take refuge here. I've had nothing to eat or drink these four days. Buggerlaus was pressing close . . . But at last, here I am – safe. Ah! I'm dying of weariness and cold. But I'd certainly like to know what became of my big fat buffoon, I mean to say my very esteemed husband. After all, did I take his money? Did I steal his bagels? Did I grab even one lousy bean?! And his money-go-mare, that was dying of hunger – it didn't see oats often, poor beast. Oh, it's a sad story. But alas! I've lost my treasure! It's at Warsaw, go fetch it who will.

PAPA TURD (*beginning to wake up*). And get Mama Turd! Cut off her years!

MAMA TURD. My God! Where am I? I must be losing my mind! But no, heavens above! —

> *Praise the Lord, I think I see*
> *Little Papa Turd asleep near me!*

Softly now. – Well, my fat old codger, did you sleep well?

PAPA TURD. Very poorly! He was good and tough, that bear! Combat of the ravenous and the cartilaginous. But the hungry have completely eaten up and devoured the stringy, as you'll see when daylight comes. D'you hear, noble Champions?

MAMA TURD. What's he babbling about? He's even stupider than when he left. Who's he talking to?

PAPA TURD. Pile, Coccyx. Answer me, pshit-sack, where are you? Oh! I'm scared. And yet, someone spoke. Who spoke? I don't suppose it was the bear. Is he back again? He's going to eat me! Pshit! Where are my matches? Oh, I lost them in battle.

MAMA TURD (*aside*). We'll take advantage of the situation and the dark. We'll pretend to be a ghost, and make him promise to pardon our pilferings.

PAPA TURD. But by Saint Anthony, someone is speaking! Leg-o'-god! Hang me if they're not.

MAMA TURD (*in a great hollow voice*). Yes, Master Turd, someone does, in fact, speak. And that archangel's trumpet which shall draw the dead from their ashes and the ultimate dust will not speak otherwise! Give ear to this stern voice. It is the voice of the Archangel Gabriel, who can give only good advice.

PAPA TURD. You don't say.

MAMA TURD. Do not interrupt me or I shall fall silent, and that means your ass in a sling.

PAPA TURD. Oh, my strumpot! I'll be quiet, I won't say another word. Continue, Madame Apparition.

MAMA TURD. We were saying, Master Turd, that you're a fat old codger.

PAPA TURD. Very fat, as a matter of fact, it's true.

MAMA TURD. Goddam it, shut up!

PAPA TURD. Oh! but angels don't swear.

MAMA TURD (aside). Pshit! (Continuing.) You are married, Mr. Turd?

PAPA TURD. Absolutely, and to the vilest of shrews.

MAMA TURD. You're trying to say that she's a charming woman.

PAPA TURD. A horror. She has fangs all over. One doesn't know how to take her.

MAMA TURD. You must take her with kindness, honored Turd, and if you do you'll see that she's at least the equal of Venus in Paradise.

PAPA TURD. Who did you say had lice?

MAMA TURD. You aren't listening, Mr. Turd. Lend us a more attentive ear. (Aside.) But I must hurry. Day is breaking. – Mr. Turd, your wife is adorable and delightful. She hasn't a single fault.

PAPA TURD. You're mistaken. There isn't a single fault she hasn't got.

MAMA TURD. Silence! Your wife has never been unfaithful to you.

PAPA TURD. I'd like to see the man that would want her. What a harpy!

MAMA TURD. She doesn't drink.

PAPA TURD. Not since I took the key to the cellar. Before that she was drunk by eight in the morning, and stank of brandy. Now that she stinks of heliotrope she doesn't smell any worse. It's all the same to me. But now I'm the only one that can get drunk.

MAMA TURD. Stupid fool ! Your wife doesn't steal your gold.

PAPA TURD. No ? That's funny.

MAMA TURD. She doesn't pinch one penny.

PAPA TURD. As witness our noble and unfortunate money-go-mare, who, not being fed for three months, had to do the entire campaign dragged by the bridle across the Ukraine. Also, he died on the job, poor beast!

MAMA TURD. All this is false. Your wife is a saint, and you, what a monster you are !

PAPA TURD. All this is true. My wife is a slut, and what a piece of tripe you are !

MAMA TURD. Take care, Papa Turd !

PAPA TURD. Yes, that's true. I forgot who I was talking to. I didn't say a word.

MAMA TURD. You killed Wenceslaus.

PAPA TURD. Well it wasn't my fault, you know. Mama Turd wanted me to.

MAMA TURD. You killed Boleslaus and Ladislaus.

PAPA TURD. So much the worse for them. They wanted to hit me.

MAMA TURD. You broke your promise to Bordure, and then you killed him too.

PAPA TURD. I'd rather it was me that was king in Lithuania than him. But right now you can see it isn't either of us. At least, you can see it isn't me.

MAMA TURD. There's only one way for all your sins to be forgiven.

PAPA TURD. What is it ? I'm willing to become a holy man. I want to be a bishop, and see my name in the calendar.

MAMA TURD. You must forgive Mama Turd for having pilfered a little gold.

PAPA TURD. Aha ! So that's it ! I'll forgive her when she gives it all back, and when I've walloped her good, and when she brings my money-go-mare back to life.

MAMA TURD. He's crazy on the subject of that horse. Oh, I'm lost ! It's getting light.

PAPA TURD. Well, anyway, I'm glad to know for sure that my dear wife has been robbing me. I have it now on the highest authority. *Omnis a Deo scientia*, which means : *Omnis*, all ; *a Deo*, knowledge ; *scientia*, comes from God. That explains the mystery. But Madame Apparition is silent. What can I do to cheer her up ? What she was saying is very amusing. Hmm, it's getting to be morning. Christ Almighty ! Now by my money-go-mare, it's Mama Turd !

MAMA TURD (*brazenly*). That's not true. I'll excommunicate you !

PAPA TURD. Carrion !

MAMA TURD. Atheist !

PAPA TURD. Oh, this is too much. I see perfectly well that it's you, you stupid bitch ! What the devil are you doing here ?

MAMA TURD. Gyron is dead and the Poles chased me out.

PAPA TURD. It was the Russians chased me. Birds of a feather flock together.

MAMA TURD. I'd say this bird met up with a jackass.

PAPA TURD. Well in a minute she's going to meet up with a palmipede. (*He throws* THE BEAR *on her.*)

MAMA TURD (*falling in a heap under the weight of* THE BEAR). Oh, God ! How awful ! Oh, I'm dying ! I'm suffocating ! It's biting me ! It's swallowing me ! It's digesting me !

PAPA TURD. It's dead, imbecile. But now that you mention it, maybe it isn't ! Oh Lord ! no, it isn't dead ! Run for our lives ! (*Getting back up on his rock.*) Our Father who art in heaven . . .

MAMA TURD (*disentangling herself*). Well, where is he ?

PAPA TURD. Oh. Lord ! She's still here. Stupid creature, isn't there any way of getting rid of her ? – Is the bear dead ?

MAMA TURD. Stupid yourself, you jackass ! He's stone cold already. How did he get here ?

PAPA TURD (*confused*). I don't know. Oh yes, now I know. He wanted to eat Pile and Coccyx, and I killed him with one blow of the Pater Noster.

MAMA TURD. Pile, Coccyx, Pater Noster! What's this all about? He's crazy, my finance!

PAPA TURD. I'm telling the exact truth, and you're the one that's crazy, you bloody ass!

MAMA TURD. Tell me the story of your campaign, Papa Turd.

PAPA TURD. Oh, Lord no! It's too long. All I know is that in spite of my incontestable valiance, everybody beat me.

MAMA TURD. What, even the Poles?

PAPA TURD. They were shouting: Long live Wenceslaus and Buggerlaus! I thought they were going to tear me to pieces. Oh, the madmen! And then they killed Rensky.

MAMA TURD. I don't give a damn! Did you know that Buggerlaus killed Champion Gyron?

PAPA TURD. I don't give a damn! And then they killed poor Lasky.

MAMA TURD. I don't give a damn!

PAPA TURD. Oh, now, wait a minute! C'mere, you carrion! Get down on your knees before your lord and master. (*He grabs her and throws her on her knees.*) You're going to undergo capital punishment.

MAMA TURD. Oh, mercy, Master Turd!

PAPA TURD. Mercy, nothing! Are you finished? Then I'll begin: twisting of the nose, pulling out of the hair, penetration of the little tip of wood into the years, extraction of the brains through the heels, laceration of the posterior, partial or even total suppression of the spinal marrow – if that's any way of removing the spininess of the character – not to mention the lancing of the floating kidney, and finally the grand beheading à la Saint John the Baptist, the whole drawn from the most sacred Scriptures of both the Old Testament and the New, set in order, corrected and perfected by yours truly, the here-present Master of Phynance. How does that suit you, chucklehead? (*He begins to lacerate her.*)

MAMA TURD. Mercy, Master Turd!

(*Loud noise at the entrance to the cave.*)

SCENE II

THE SAME. *Enter* BUGGERLAUS

BUGGERLAUS (*rushing into the cave with his soldiers*). Forward, my friends! Up with Poland!

PAPA TURD. Oh, oh! Just a moment, Mr. Polander. Wait till I'm through with Madame my better half.

BUGGERLAUS (*striking him*). Take that, coward, beggar, bully, infidel, Mohammedan!

PAPA TURD (*blow for blow*). Take that! Polack, drunkard, bastard, dastard, hussard, tartard, scabbard, snothard, savoyard, Communist!

MAMA TURD (*hitting him too*). Take that! capon, porkon, felon, histrion, scullion, rascaglion, Polack!

(*The soldiers throw themselves on the* TURDS, *who defend themselves as best they can.*)

PAPA TURD. Gad! they're beating us hollow.

MAMA TURD. What feet these Polacks have!

PAPA TURD. Now by my green candle, isn't this ever going to end? Another one! Oh, if I only had my money-go-mare!

BUGGERLAUS. Hit 'em! Hit 'em again!

VOICES (*offstage*):
> God save our Papa Turd,
> Our gracious Phynancier . . .

PAPA TURD. Hurray! They're here! Here come the Turdsmen. Forward, Gentlemen of Phynance, come on! We need you!

(*Enter* THE CHAMPIONS, *who throw themselves into the fray.*)

COCCYX. Out you go, Polacks!

PILE. Hey! Mister Phynance! We meet again. Forward! Press forward! To the door! Once outside, all we have to do is run for it.

PAPA TURD. Yes, I'm good at that. – Oh! he hit me!

BUGGERLAUS. My God! I'm wounded!

STANISLAS LECZINSKI. It's nothing, Sire.

BUGGERLAUS. No, I'm only stunned.

JAN SOBIESKI. Hit 'em! Keep hitting 'em! They're getting away, the scoundrels!

COCCYX. We're almost there! Follow me, boys. In consequeynt of the fact thatte I see daylight.

PILE. Courage, Sir Turd!

PAPA TURD. Oh yes, I'm filling my pants – with courage. Forward, hornstrumpot! Murdder 'em, massacre 'em, skin 'em alive, draw blood! Turdhorn! Ah, they're falling back.

COCCYX. There's only two left guarding the door.

PAPA TURD (knocking them down with THE BEAR). One! . . . and two! Oof! here I am, outside! All right, the rest of you, let's go! Follow me, and fast!

SCENE III

The backdrop shows the province of Livonia covered with snow.

THE TURDS *and their suite in flight.*

PAPA TURD. Well, I guess they've given up trying to catch us.

MAMA TURD. Yes, Buggerlaus has gone to get himself crowned.

PAPA TURD. I certainly don't envy him that crown.

MAMA TURD. And you're right, Papa Turd. [You'd do better to come with me. This is not a peaceful country. Let's leave. Let's profit by the fact that we're on the seashore, and board the first ship out. But where to go?

PAPA TURD. Where to go, Mama Turd? *Quo vadimus?*
That's easy – to France! . . . That's where we'll live from
now on, Mama Turd.

MAMA TURD. Bravo, Papa Turd. On, to France!

PAPA TURD. I see a ship approaching. We're saved!]

(*They disappear into the distance.*)

SCENE IV

The bridge of a ship running close to shore
on the Baltic.

On the bridge, PAPA TURD *and all his crew.*

THE CAPTAIN. Ah, what a fine breeze!

PAPA TURD. Yes, we're sailing along with a rapidity border-
ing on the miraculous, and that's a fact. We must be making
at least a million knots an hour, and the nice thing about these
knots is that once they're made they can't be unmade. Of
course, it's true we have the wind in the poop.

PILE. What an imbecile!

(*A squall comes up. The ship dips*
and churns up the sea.)

PAPA TURD. Oh, my God! We've capsized! Everything is
upside down. Hey, Captain, the boat is sinking!

THE CAPTAIN. Everybody to leeward. Furl the foresail!

PAPA TURD. Oh, for God's sake, no! Don't all rush to one
side. That's most imprudent. Suppose the wind should suddenly change – we'll all go to the bottom and the fish'll eat
us.

THE CAPTAIN. Don't pull in! Press close and full.

PAPA TURD. Hey, sure pull in! Pull in! I'm in a hurry, you

hear me? It's your fault, you louse of a captain, if we don't pull in. We should have been there long ago. All right, I'll take over now. Clear the tack! Heave to, for God's sake! Drop the anchor. Tack about! Fore! Aft! Hoist the sails, drop the sails! Helm up, helm down, helm in the middle! You see? – everything is going fine. Now heave to in the trough of the sea, and that'll be perfect.

(*They all roar. The breeze freshens.*)

THE CAPTAIN. Haul in the standing-jib and take a reef in the tops'l!

PAPA TURD. That's it! That's good! You hear, Mr. Crew? Haul in the standing jock and take a crap in the focs'l. (*They die laughing. A wave washes on board.*) Oh, what a deluge! This is what comes of the orders I gave.

MAMA TURD (*to* PILE). Delightful, this navigation.

(*A second wave washes over.*)

PILE (*drowning*). I renounce Satan and all his pumps!

PAPA TURD. Ho, boy! Get us a drink.

(*All sit and drink.*)

MAMA TURD. Ah, how delightful it will be to see beautiful France once more – our old friends, our castle of Mountdragon.

PAPA TURD. Yes, we'll soon be there. And right now we're coming to the castle of Elsinore.

PILE. How happy I'll be to see my beloved Spain again.

COCCYX. Yes, and we'll amaze our countrymen with tales of our marvellous adventures.

PAPA TURD. Oh, absolutely. And as for me, I'm going to have myself appointed Master of Phynance at Paris.

MAMA TURD. That's right! – Oh! what hit us?

COCCYX. It's nothing. We're just rounding the point at Elsinore.

PILE. And now our noble barque hurls itself full sail over the dark waves of the Northern Sea.

PAPA TURD. That wild, inhospitable sea that washes the shores of Germany – so called because all the inhabitants are cousins-german.

MAMA TURD. Now that's what I call erudition. They say it's a very beautiful country.

PAPA TURD. Yes, gentlemen, but however beautiful it may be, it can't compare with Poland. Because if there weren't any Poland, there wouldn't be any Poles!

THE END